EASTER STARRING EGG!

W9-BEV-745

written by
CYNTHIA PLATT

illustrated by
LEIRE MARTÍN

HOUGHTON MIFFLIN HARCOURT
Boston ★ New York

Easter morning! Oh what a day!
Egg's all ready for the *par-tay*.

TO THE
EASTER EGG
HUNT

This is the time when all eggs go to hide.
Egg is egg-cited to be here outside!

Egg is special. Egg has *finesse.*
Egg's look strives for more—never less!

Covered in glitter and covered in glue,
All fancied up for the big *rendezvous!*

Egg hunt starting—ready, set, GO!
Egg looks on, his shell all aglow.

EASTER
EGG
HUNT

GO!

**Egg is all decked out and here is the reason:
It's clear that this will be *his* Easter season.**

Wow,
those bonnets!

Hip straw hats, too!

One is *his* kid.
But which one?
Who?

Some kids move quickly and some at an amble,
Hunting for eggs in a fantastic scramble!

EGGS

Kids are sprinting, cheering so loud!
Egg knows he'll stand out from the crowd

He doesn't mind all the stomping like thunder
As kids search 'round for eggs they can plunder.

Shell by shell, his friends are selected,
Sad when Egg is still not collected.

One from his carton gets
plucked from the clover.
"Quick, Egg!" she says.
"The hunt's almost over!"

Egg says *ta-ta* with a big smile.
He knows he'll get found in a while!

His kid will come, they'll be one of a kind.
But Egg's friends call out, "Don't get left behind!"

Sure he's last, but Egg doesn't worry.
His kid wouldn't be in a hurry!

Egg is just magic, he can't help but show it . . .

He thinks the right kid will
see him and know it!

Wow, this new kid could be the one!
They tell Egg, "Oh, my hunt is done!"

Finally Egg is so perfectly matched—
A fun new friendship at long last has hatched!